Originally published in Dutch as *Flut, mijn boek in de put* in the series
"De Lettertuin," copyright © 1997 by Bakermat Uitgevers,
Mechelen, Belgium. All rights reserved.

Published in the U.S. in 2002 by Big Tent Entertainment,
216 West 18th Street, New York, New York 10011.

ISBN: 1-59226-048-9

Printed in China.

Listening to Stories

By
Eva de Wilde

Buried Treasure

Illustrated by
Veerle Derave

BIG TENT ENTERTAINMENT

A Game

"I've got you now, villain!"
says Jeff.
"You'll never get away!"
He ties Bob to the trunk
of their favorite tree.

"You're wrong!"
Bob says.
"I'll find a way to escape!"

Jeff likes this game.
It's just like the movies.

"I'm going to find
the other villain now,"
he tells Bob.
"I'll be back!"
He runs off to look
for their friend Anne.

"*Pssst*," says Bob.
Anne pops out
from behind the tree.
She unties Bob.
They sneak away.

"Stop, villains!" cries Jeff.

Homework

The game is over.
Bob is Bob again.
Jeff is Jeff again.

"That looked like fun,"
says Jeff's neighbor, Pete.
"It was," says Jeff.

"Time for homework!"
Mom calls out.

"Yuck," says Jeff.
Today's homework is to read
a book called *Tom and Max*.

Jeff reads,

This is Tom.
He has a dog named Max.
Max is missing.
Tom looks in the house.
Tom looks in the garden.
Max is gone.
Tom is sad.

"This is boring,"
grumbles Jeff.
"I hate reading!"

Jeff puts *Tom and Max*
in a plastic bag.
He goes outside
and digs a hole in the yard.
Then Jeff drops the book
in the hole—
and covers it up with dirt!

"Good-bye, book!"
says Jeff.

No Book, No Worries

It's noisy in the classroom.
Jessica is throwing paper airplanes.
Ben is tipping back in his chair.

Oops, here comes the teacher!
"In your seats, everyone!"
calls Miss Brown.

"Who's going to read today?"
Miss Brown asks.
"Eve, will you start?"

Eve reads out loud
from *Tom and Max*.
"Very good,"
says Miss Brown.
"Now it's your turn, Jeff."

"I don't have my book,"
says Jeff.
Miss Brown frowns.
"Where is it?" she asks.

"It's—it's gone,"
Jeff answers.
The class laughs.
Miss Brown frowns again.
"Laurie, please read for us,"
she says.

Jeff is happy.
Everything seems okay.
No book, no worries.
The bell rings for recess.
"Stay here, Jeff,"
says Miss Brown.
Uh-oh!

"What's wrong?"
Miss Brown asks him.
"Why didn't you bring
your book today?"

"I don't like reading,"
says Jeff.
"It's boring!
I'd rather play games."

"Sometimes reading a book
is as much fun as playing a game,"
Miss Brown tells him.
"That's impossible!" says Jeff.

Miss Brown laughs.
"If I can prove it to you,
you owe me a bag of lollipops.
If I can't, I owe you
a bag of lollipops.
How about it?"
"It's a bet!" says Jeff.

"Good," says Miss Brown.
"Now go out for recess.
And don't forget—
bring back *Tom and Max* tomorrow."

At the end of the day,
Miss Brown gives Jeff a package.
He takes it home,
but he doesn't look inside.
Instead, he goes over to Bob's house.

"Come on, let's play soccer,"
Jeff says.
"Not now," says Bob.
"I'm reading a really funny book."

"Come on," Jeff says again.
But Bob won't budge.

Jeff goes home.
He peeks in Miss Brown's package.
Inside, there's a book
with a note that says,
"Read until you find one silly word."

The book is about a superhero.
The hero can't use his powers until
he hears someone say "tigglemuffin."

"I guess that's the silly word,"
thinks Jeff.
He could stop reading now,
but he decides to read
a little more.

Now the hero is chasing a villain.
He needs someone to say
the word!
"Muffintiggle," says an old lady.
"Tifflemuggin," says a little boy.
"No!" yells the hero.
"It's tigglemuffin!"

Jeff laughs.
What a crazy story!
He keeps reading.
Before he knows it,
he has read the whole book!

Buried Treasure

The next morning, before school,
Jeff goes out to search
for *Tom and Max*.

"Aha!" says Jeff.
"Here's the bag I put it in."
But the bag is empty!
Jeff's neighbor walks by.
"What's the matter, Jeff?"

Jeff tells Pete about his
missing book.
"Come with me," says Pete.

Pete takes Jeff to his garden.
"Did you know there's
a buried treasure here?"
says Pete.
Jeff isn't sure he believes Pete.
But he starts to dig.

Soon he spots something.
It's a bag with a book in it.
Tom and Max!

"Hey, that's mine!" says Jeff.
Pete smiles.
Then he asks,
"Jeff, why on earth did you
bury your book?"

"I didn't like it," says Jeff.
"I thought I didn't like
to read at all.
But then I read another book,
and it was good!"

"I know what you mean,"
Pete says.
"There are some books I like,
and some books I don't.
Once you find one that's right for
you, reading is fun."

"Yeah," says Jeff.
"*Really* fun!"

Suddenly Jeff laughs.
"I better go," he says.
"I have to stop at the candy store
on my way to school.
I owe my teacher a bag of
lollipops!"